GIBBET HILL

GIBBET HILL

GIBBET HILL

BRAM STOKER

Annotated Edition

WILDSIDE PRESS

Originally published in 1890.
First reprinted 2024.

CONTENTS

A NOTE ON THE TEXT .7

INTRODUCTION: BRAM STOKER. 9

GIBBET HILL. 11

A NOTE ON THE TEXT

This story originally appeared in the *Supplement to the Daily Express* (Dublin, Ireland), Wednesday, December 17, 1890. It was recently discovered by a researcher looking into the works of Bram Stoker, the author of *Dracula*, and was a previously unknown horror story by this famous author.

It seems particularly apt to make it generally available just in time for Halloween.

This version has been lightly edited, primarily to correct typos, accidentally dropped words, and standardize punctuation. British spelling has been retained, of course. The few archaic words Stoker used, such as "cachinnation" (loud, boisterous, or excessive laughter), have been retained, as the author intended them.

INTRODUCTION: BRAM STOKER

Bram Stoker (1847–1912) was an Irish author best known for his groundbreaking work in horror and mystery literature. Born in Dublin, Stoker overcame a childhood illness to become a passionate writer. He later moved to London, where he managed the Lyceum Theatre, working closely with famed actor Sir Henry Irving. While theater management occupied much of his professional life, it was his foray into fiction that left a lasting mark on literature.

Stoker is most famous for his 1897 Gothic horror novel *Dracula*, which introduced the iconic vampire character Count Dracula. The novel skillfully blends mystery, terror, and supernatural themes, creating a narrative that has captivated readers for generations. Beyond *Dracula*, Stoker wrote several other works of horror and suspense, including *The Jewel of Seven Stars* and *The Lair of the White Worm*. These stories often featured ancient curses, eerie atmospheres, and dark, brooding villains.

Stoker's contribution to the horror genre lies in his ability to merge folklore and Gothic conventions with modern fears, creating tales of suspense that continue to influence horror and mystery writers today. His legacy endures as one of the most significant figures in supernatural fiction.

GIBBET HILL

When I left the Royal Huts Inn, on the top of Hindhead,[1] in order to visit the Devil's Punch Bowl[2] and Gibbet Hill,[3] immortalized by Turner in the *Liber Studiorium*,[4] I passed along a wide straight

---

1   The Witley side of Hindhead refers to the area around the village of Witley and its proximity to Hindhead, a high ridge and large expanse of heathland in the Surrey Hills, part of an Area of Outstanding Natural Beauty (AONB). Hindhead, located close to the village of Witley, is most famous for the Devil's Punch Bowl, a large natural amphitheater, and one of the most stunning landscapes in southern England. This side of Hindhead offers a rich combination of scenic beauty, history, and outdoor activities.

Witley itself is a historic village with roots going back to the Saxon period. It has several notable buildings, including Witley Church (St. James), which dates back to the 12th century and contains remarkable medieval wall paintings. The surrounding countryside is lush and forested, with Witley Common offering walking paths and opportunities to explore the area's natural beauty.

2   The Devil's Punch Bowl is a large natural amphitheater located near Hindhead in Surrey, England. It's part of the Surrey Hills Area of Outstanding Natural Beauty and one of the most striking landscapes in southern England. The bowl is a deep, circular valley formed by erosion, surrounded by heathland, woods, and dramatic ridges, making it a popular spot for walkers and nature lovers.

The Devil's Punch Bowl is steeped in folklore. One popular legend suggests that the bowl was formed by the devil himself. According to the tale, the devil became so angry with the people of Thorpe, a nearby village, that he scooped out a giant handful of earth to throw at them, creating the deep hollow in the process. Another version of the legend claims that the devil and the god Thor engaged in a battle here, with Thor's hammer causing the distinctive shape of the Punch Bowl.

Historically, the Devil's Punch Bowl was an isolated and notorious area for highwaymen and bandits in the 18th and 19th centuries. The most infamous event linked to the area was the 1786 murder of a sailor by three men, who were subsequently captured, tried, and hanged near the site. The "Sailor's Stone" near the Punch Bowl commemorates the event and serves as a somber reminder of its past.

3   Gibbet Hill has a grim historical reputation, primarily due to its association with the execution of criminals. Its name comes from the "gibbet," a type of gallows used for hanging. In the 18th century, it was a place where highwaymen and criminals were hanged, and their bodies were displayed as a deterrent to others. One of the most famous events tied to the hill was the 1786 murder of a sailor by three men. The three murderers were hanged on Gibbet Hill, near the spot where they committed the crime, and their bodies were left in iron cages to serve as a warning to others. This gruesome practice was intended to make an example of those who defied the law, though it was discontinued in later years.

4   The *Liber Studiorum* is a series of landscape prints created by the English painter J.M.W. Turner between 1807 and 1819. Turner designed this collection to showcase different categories of landscape art and to illustrate his mastery across various styles. The title *Liber Studiorum* (meaning "Book of Studies") was inspired by Claude Lorrain's *Liber Veritatis*, which similarly cataloged landscape art.

Turner's *Liber Studiorum* includes 71 prints, divided into six main types of landscape:

road—the new high road between London and Portsmouth—and shortly came to the edge of the Punch Bowl and feasted my eyes on its beauty. The fog, which had been heavy in London when I left on this mid-October morning, extended even to Haslemere[5] and hung in the valleys so that the tops of the Surrey hills rose like islands from the sea of mist, and in the brilliant sunshine which glorified these upper levels, softened and mellowed all the wide expanse of hill and dale and down which ranged between me and the Southern coast. The hill gave steeply on all sides save the north-west, where the circular valley opened to the plain below. All the summer tints were chastened and mellowed; all the full colours which the sunshine had glorified had faded into the sere of Autumn. The pink and purple of the heather were changed to a brown with only a suggestion of faded colour to warm its tone. The bracken was of rich amber and faded yellow, and the myriads of grasses and wildflowers had donned their winter garb—the hues of decay.

Through all this rich mass of Autumn tints, the broom, untouched as yet by the frost, sent an emerald flash. The green bushes which fringed the tiny stream running through the valley seemed of supernatural vividness, and the dark green of the pines which covered the western slope and ran down into the valley seemed to assert in some positive way the right of nature to maintain her own colour despite all influences. Away to the north and west, past the spurs and shoulders of the hill, the woods and valleys, the copses and villages and

historical, pastoral, mountainous, marine, architectural, and epic. Each print began as a sketch by Turner, which was then engraved by professional printmakers. The series was intended as both a teaching tool for students of landscape painting and a statement of Turner's artistic skill, as he believed that landscape painting could be as serious and complex as history painting.

Though the *Liber Studiorum* was not completed as Turner initially envisioned, it remains an important part of his legacy and an influential work in the history of British landscape art.

5   Haslemere is a small market town in Surrey, England, known for its picturesque setting and historical charm. Located near the borders of Hampshire and West Sussex, Haslemere lies within the Surrey Hills Area of Outstanding Natural Beauty (AONB). Its surrounding countryside features rolling hills, woodlands, and heathlands, making it popular for walking, hiking, and outdoor activities.

The town has a history that stretches back to the Middle Ages and was primarily a rural, agricultural area. Its growth accelerated in the 19th century with the arrival of the railway, which connected it to London, making it a desirable location for commuters. The town retains much of its historic character, with many old buildings, including traditional timber-framed houses and Georgian architecture.

hills and ridges ranged in endless succession; and it was after a long, long pause that I turned from drinking in the beauty of the scene with my heart full of the power and majesty and purifying influence of nature's beauty. "Here at least," said I to myself, "the soul of man is elevated; and on this higher plane of natures' handiwork the evil of our hearts is lulled."

As I turned, however, I started, for, as if by the irony of fate, there, beside me, was a grim memorial of man's wickedness and lust for blood—a tombstone[6] by the roadside, marking the spot where a century ago a poor seaman trudging on his way from Portsmouth was murdered.

But not the stone only was of interest; for by it were three figures which would have arrested attention anywhere. They were only children, but of types that were not common. Two were young Indian girls of an age which by the slower development of English girlhood would be about some thirteen or fourteen years; being, however, of Eastern birth, they were probably much younger. They stood one on each side of the memorial stone, looking almost like heraldic supporters, as each with a slim brown hand resting on an elbow of the stone, leaned her face on the hand while looking at me gravely with long, dark, fathomless eyes. They were both very pretty of their type, and their slim girlish figures were draped m black of some shimmering material, made in a half Eastern fashion with a wide belt of the stuff round the waist, and some kind of dark material wound around the head and acting as a head gear. The third of the group was a little boy of some ten years old, with hair of spun gold, eyes like blue porcelain, and a winning smile on his rosy face. One might designate him indifferently a Cupid or an angel. He was dressed in a dark blood-coloured tunic.

For a few seconds I stood looking at this group, they regarding me steadfastly without the slightest movement. Then I spoke to them, making some remark about the beauty of the scene.

One of the girls said, tapping the stone with her hand as she spoke: "Can you tell us anything about this stone, sir? We are strangers."

---

6   A short walk from the summit of Gibbet Hill is the "Sailor's Stone," a memorial marking the site where the sailor, believed to be a victim of a notorious murder, was killed. The stone is engraved with inscriptions commemorating the event and serves as a reminder of the darker side of the area's history.

"I am a stranger here myself, but I think we will find it here," I answered, as I proceeded to read the inscription, which is on both sides of the stone. When I read of the word murder, they all three looked at each other and then at me, and shuddered, and, strange to say, followed the shudder with a smile, I thought they might be frightened, and I hastened to add, "But you need not let this disturb you. It all happened a hundred years ago, when the country was very different from what it is now."

One of the girls said in a low voice, whose tones were peculiarly penetrating:

"I hope not—I trust not," and the little boy looked up at me with a laugh and said:

"I suppose if there were a murder now, someone would be stuck up on Gibbet Hill!"

"Hullo, young man," said I. "You know all about it, I see. I am going up to the hilltop to see the Memorial Cross. Will you come and see where they put the murderers?"

"With pleasure," he said, with an air of almost supernatural gravity, lifting his cap in acknowledgment of my invitation. The girls bowed too, and we all moved up the hill together. As we went, I noticed that the boy had one of his hands tightly clenched.

"What have you got there?" I asked him.

"These," he said, opening his hand and showing me a crumpled mass of great earthworms, wriggling in their sudden freedom. "I love worms," he went on. "See, they wriggle so, and you can pull them out long!" and he illustrated the latter fact.

"Poor worms!" said I. "Why not let them go? They would much rather be on the ground."

"Shan't," was his only reply, as he shoved them into the folds of his tunic.

There were a lot of persons at the cross when we reached the top of Gibbet Hill, besides abundant evidence of recent visitors in the shape of eggshells and pieces of newspaper—for the cross is a favourite picnicking spot. Amongst the strangers my fancy was chiefly taken by a lady and gentleman whom I dubbed "the honeymoon couple." I soon became so absorbed by the lovely view which lay stretched before me—a wilderness of rising hilltops with green woods and rich valleys—that I quite forgot my young companions. I went to the edge of the steep hill and sat down looking eastwards and lost myself in the beauty of the scene.

Presently I remembered my young companions and looked around for them, but they had quite disappeared; there was not a sight of them anywhere around.

My departure from London had been early, and the walk from Haslemere in the blazing October sun a little fatiguing, so, after a while, when I had been all around the summit of the Head and had, so to speak, boxed the scenic compass, I took my way to a deep shady grove of hazel and beech with tall pines rising over all—one of those dense copses that creep up from the valley, throwing jagged spikes of greenery up the slopes of the hill. Here there was the very perfection of autumn fulness. The undergrowth grew luxuriantly under the shelter of the clustering pines. The brown of the bark and the blueish bloom of the foliage of the pines, as one gazed into the half dim aisles between them—the sweet aromatic odour which they exhaled—the sleepy silence, accentuated only by the hum of nature's myriad vitalities—the soft, rich grass, whose summer greenery stood untouched as yet in this sheltered dell—all invited to repose. With a blissful feeling of content, I stretched myself on the grass, and soon lost my thoughts and my consciousness in the interlaced branches above me.

How long I slept I know not; but it must have been a good while, for I felt thoroughly refreshed as to brain, and with that half-aching sense of cramped muscles which comes after a long period of unchanged attitude; and there was over me that mysterious sense of elapsed time which tells philosophers that our thought is continuous in some form or another. There was, however, no sense of duty omitted—no press of coming work, which in such cases destroys the charm of awaking. I knew that there was ample time before me, and that I might muse on, unchecked, that I could revel to my heart's content in the sense of freedom, arid enjoy the freshness and purity of the air in this wonderful spot.

And so I did not stir, but lay on my back with my hands under my head looking up into the branches and watching the gleams of light struggle through the tracery of leaf and branch. I thought of many things, in that luxurious half dreamy way which belongs to the leisure of an habitually busy man. Taking up a thread of thought and dropping it again—swaying between general and particular ideas—in all ways realizing that greatest of pleasures, intellectual *laissez aller.*[7]

There was in the air the same faint hum of varied sounds which had at the first lulled me to sleep; but somehow the volume was richer than before—fuller and satisfying to the ear, and with a special significance, as if not only all nature was speaking but that there was some one voice amongst the myriad more potent than the rest. I listened with a growing interest, and the sound seemed to take a more definite place amongst nature's harmonies. It was not as if it grew in loudness, but merely as if the vibrations accumulated, coming in waves more quickly than they could die away.

Gradually all the other noises seemed to die away, and I heard only this one sound. It seemed to be closer and closer as I began to distinguish more clearly, until I shortly came to the conclusion that its source was separated from me by only some score of yards. Then I began to be able to analyse it a little. In general effect it was like a sort of musical muffled corncrake—a corncrake in a whisper—but with some subtle prevailing sweetness which seemed of almost irresistible attraction. Presently I raised my head from amongst the bracken where I lay and looked whence the sound proceeded.

There, to my surprise, in an open dell where the light fell through a break in the trees, were grouped the children whom I had seen. The two girls were seated, and between them the little boy stood up. One of the girls held in her left hand something which looked like a set of Pan pipes made of thin canes but slightly thicker than wheaten straws. Across this she drew something attached to the fingers of the right hand, which made the bass of the strange corncrake sound. The other girl held a shell with strings across it which she touched lightly; and the boy had a sort of reed flute which gave forth a peculiarly long sweet note, but which blended in the mass of music. Then the girls joined in a sort of monotonous chant of strange sweetness but very,

---

7   Intellectual *laissez-aller* refers to a state of mental laxity or carelessness, where someone allows their thoughts and reasoning to become undisciplined, unfocused, or overly relaxed. It comes from the French term *laissez-aller*, which literally means "let go" or "let things take their course." In this context, it implies an abandonment of rigorous thought or a lack of critical thinking.

Someone experiencing intellectual *laissez-aller* might not challenge their assumptions, fail to evaluate ideas critically, or let their reasoning be driven by emotion or whim rather than careful analysis. It's often used as a critique of superficial or lazy thinking, particularly when deeper inquiry or intellectual discipline is required.

very faint. They were all three looking well to one side of me. By and by the girls stood up; they all turned slightly, and I could see that they were evidently turning slowly in a complete circle, as though seeking in every direction around them. As they began to face my direction, I sank down again into the bracken so that they might not see me, for the affair began to absorb my interest. I took care, however, to peep through the fronds of the bracken and see all that went on. A very short time elapsed before my attention was diverted, and in not the most pleasant of ways.

Hearing a stir and rustle among the dead leaves beside me I looked round, and almost jumped to my feet, for there close by, and approaching closer, was a large snake of the blindworm species.[8] It came straight towards me and actually passed over my feet. I did not stir, and it went on, heeding me no more than if I had been a log of wood, and wriggled away towards the group in the sunlit glade. It was evidently attracted by the strange, weird music, and as this was my first actual experience of serpent—charming my interest grew, and I watched the little party more closely than before. They went on with their music, and the snake approached closer and closer; till at the feet of the lair-haired child it stopped, and, curling itself into a spiral, raised its head and began to hiss. The boy looked down, and the girls turned their eyes towards him, but the music did not stop for a moment; on the contrary, it grew something quicker. Then the snake twined itself around the child's ankle and began to climb its way up his body, wriggling round and round his leg and thigh, and up and up, till at last it crawled along the arm that held the flute.

Then, suddenly, the music stopped. The two girls stood up, and the boy stretched out his arm with the snake wound around it, with

---

8   The blindworm, also known as the slow worm (*Anguis fragilis*), is a legless reptile that resembles a small snake but is actually a type of lizard. It is native to Europe and parts of Asia and is most commonly found in grasslands, gardens, and woodland edges.

Despite its snake-like appearance, the blindworm has several characteristics that identify it as a lizard. For example, it has eyelids and can blink, unlike snakes, and it can also shed its tail as a defense mechanism, a common trait among lizards. Blindworms are called "blind" because of the old belief that they were sightless, but in reality, they have small, functional eyes.

Slow worms can grow up to 50 centimeters (about 20 inches) in length, and their smooth, shiny skin can vary in color, from brown or copper to grey. They are mostly active at dusk and dawn, feeding on insects, slugs, and other small invertebrates. Blindworms are non-venomous and are generally harmless to humans.

Despite being fairly widespread, slow worms are often elusive and spend much of their time hiding under rocks, logs, or in compost heaps, which makes them less visible than other lizards or reptiles.

his hand stretched out wide open, the palm upwards. The snake remained perfectly still, as if transformed into stone. Then the girls took hands and circled slowly around the boy, uttering a low, whispering, mysterious chant, something the same as the earlier one, but this time in decrescendo as compared with the former crescendo, and in a minor key. This went on for quite two or three minutes. The boy remained perfectly still, with his arm extended, and his blue eyes fixed on the snake. Then the latter raised its head slightly and seemed to follow with it the movements of the circling girls.

They continued their slow movement, round and round, the snake's movements being more and more pronounced with each revolution, till presently it was boldly turning, like the automatic motion of a firework, around the boy's arm. Gradually the motion of the girls got slower and that of the snake correspondingly less, till, presently, the girls' movement, and the low crooning music, which had never stopped, died away altogether, and the snake hung, a dead mass as limp as a piece of string, across the boy's hand. The boy never moved, but the girls let go each others' hands, and one of them, who had stopped just in front of the boy, took the snake by head and tail and seemed to gently pull it out straight. When she let it go, it lay across the boy's hand as stiff as a piece of wood.

There was something uncanny about this which recalled to me recollections of a man whom I had once seen in a cataleptic fit, and whose body retained any position into which it was put, no matter how grotesque or how uncomfortable or strained. The snake seemed to be under some similar condition, and with strange curiosity I awaited the next development. The boy continued impassive his hand still stretched out and the snake resting across it. The girls stood a little in front of and on either side of him, so that the outstretched hand was midway between them.

Then began some questioning between them in a language which I presumed to be some form of Indian, but which I did not understand. Both voices were sweet, with a peculiar penetrating power, but one of them I seemed instinctively to fear, although it was the sweeter and softer of the two. Somehow—and the idea was quite spontaneous—it seemed to suggest murder. From the tones and inflections of the voices, I gathered that all utterances were put in the form of questions—a supposition shortly confirmed in a strange way, for the answers were given by the rigid snake. When each girl in turn had had her say—and they suggested positive and negative in their tones—the snake would slowly turn around like the needle in a compass and point its head to either one. The sweeter voice seemed to be the positive, and the other the negative in the inquiry; and in all the earlier questions the snake, after turning slowly around, remained with its head towards the negative. This first seemed to disturb and then annoy the positive inquirer, and her voice grew more deadly sweet and penetrating until it made me shudder. Then she seemed to get more and more enraged, for her eyes gleamed with a dark unholy light, and at the last came her question in a keen, thrilling whisper. For answer, the snake then spun round quicker and quicker and suddenly came to a dead stop in front of the other girl.

The disappointed one gave one fierce, short, sharp sound like a dog's bark, whilst a look of deadly malice swept over her face and then passed away, leaving it as serene as before. At the same instant, the rigidity of the snake collapsed, and it hung for an instant as limp as before, and then slipped to the ground, and lay there all in a heap without motion, as if dead. The boy started, as though from sleep to waking, and began to laugh. The girls joined in the cachinnation[9], and in an instant the glade, which had seemed so weird, grew instinct with laughter, as the children chased each other into the recesses of the wood, and disappeared from view.

Then I rose up from the bracken where I lay. I could hardly believe my eyes and thought that I must have been sleeping and had dreamt it all. But there lay the seemingly dead snake before me as palpable evidence that I had beheld the events.

* * * *

The sun was far in the west when I had finished my stroll through the laneways and copses upon the Witley side of Hindhead and found myself once more at its highest point on Gibbet Hill.

The place was now deserted. The picnickers had all gone home; the pony traps and donkeys and parties of school children had disappeared, and nothing remained of the day's visitation but the usual increase in old newspapers and broken eggshells. As the light was just beginning to fade and the air to grow a shade colder, the sense of loneliness was more than ever marked. But I had come from the

9   loud, boisterous, or excessive laughter

midst of the hum and turmoil of the city to enjoy this very loneliness, and its luxury was to me unspeakable. Down in the valleys the mist still lay dim and fleecy white, and from it the hilltops rose dark and grim. A belt of cloud fringed the whole horizon, and above it stretched a sea of sulfur yellow, flecked here and there with little clouds of white which, swimming high above the level of the hill, caught the last splendours of the sun, now obscured by the horizon. One or two stars began to twinkle through the darkening sky, and a stillness that seemed sentient stole up through the valley and reached to where I sat.

Then the air grew colder, and the silence became perfect. The stars swam out into the sky, which had now a darker blue, and a soft light fell on the scene. I sat on and on and drank in the wondrous beauty in which I was immersed. Weariness of mind and body seemed of the dim past, and as if they could never again be other than a sad memory. In such moments a man seems almost to be born again, and to have every faculty renewed to the full. I leaned with my back against the great stone cross, and, putting my hands behind me, clasped my arms around its back so as to change my position and be able to enjoy more fully the luxury of rest.

Suddenly, without a word of warning, each hand was grasped from behind and held tight in a pair of hands, thin and warm but so strong that I could make no movement; and at the same time a scarf or shawl of some light, fleecy, but thick material was thrown over my face and drawn tightly from behind, holding my head close to the stone. So pinioned and gagged, I could neither move nor speak and had perforce to await the coming events. Then my hands were tied with a string put around the wrists and drawn tight, so that I was fixed more firmly than before. I could hear no sound and took it for granted that I was being prepared for robbery. I was alone, far away from everyone, and in the hands of men stronger than I was myself, and so resigned myself to the situation as well as I could—secretly thankful that I had only a small sum of money with me. After a time, which seemed long, but which was probably of but a few minutes' duration, the scarf was pulled down so far that my eyes were free, though my mouth was still covered and I was unable to cry out.

For a few moments I was too surprised even to think as strange what i saw before me. Instead of burly footpads with rude manner and coarse force, there were the three children who had arrested my attention earlier in the day. They stood before me perfectly still and silent for a little while, their eyes being the only features which expressed either consciousness or interest of any kind. Two of them, the boy and one girl, then smiled on me with an amused superiority, whilst the other—she who in the glade had exhibited such anger—smiled with a deadly cold hate which, bound as I was, made me shudder. This latter then approached me closer, the others remaining quite still and looking on with their superior amused smile. She took from her waist, where it was concealed in the folds of her dress, a long sharp dagger, thin, double-edged, and lethal-looking. This she proceeded to flourish before me with extraordinary dexterity and rapidity. Half the time its keen edge actually touched my skin, and the contact made me wince. Anon she would dart towards my eyes till I could feel its cold point actually touching my eyeballs. Then she would hurl herself at me with the point of the deadly weapon directed to my heart, but would stop just as it seemed that my last moment had come. This went on for a little while; but short though it was it seemed endless. I felt a cold chill, a strange numbness, growing over me; my heart seemed to get cold and weak—colder and colder—weaker and weaker, still, till at length my eyes closed. I tried to open them—succeeded; tried again—failed, succeeded failed—and at length consciousness, passed away from me.

The last thing I remember seeing with my waking eyes was the gleam of the long knife in the starlight as it moved in the young girl's dexterous play. The last sound I heard was a low laugh from all three of the children.

* * * *

The voice in my ears was dim and distant; but it gradually grew louder, and the spoken words became intelligible:

"Wake up!—Wake up, man! You will get your death of cold!"

Cold! The word struck home, for there was at my heart a numbness, and a chill as of death. My consciousness struggled back into existence, and I opened my eyes.

It was now much brighter, for a great yellow moon had arisen, and the common was flooded with its light. Beside me were two persons whom at once I recognized as "the honeymoon couple" of earlier in the day. The man was bending over me, and was shaking me roughly by the shoulder, whilst the lady stood by, looking on anxiously, with her hands clasped.

"He is not dead, George, is he?" I heard her say. The answer came.

"No, I thank goodness!—He must have fallen asleep. It is a mercy that you had the inspiration to come out to see the moonlight view from here; he might have died of cold. See! The ground is white with the hoar-frost already. Wake up, man!—Wake up, and come away!"

"My heart," I murmured, "My heart!" for it was icy cold.

The man looked more serious, and said to his wife—

"Bella, this may be serious. Could you run back to the hotel and send someone if necessary? It may be that his heart is affected."

"Certainly, dear; shall I go at once?"

"Wait a minute first." He leant over me again. The past was coming back to me quickly, and I asked him:

"Did you see anywhere some children, two Indian girls, and a fair-haired boy?"

"Yes! Hours and hours ago, as they went down the London road on a tricycle. They were laughing, and we thought them the prettiest and happiest children we had ever seen. But why?"

"My heart! My heart!" I cried out again, for there was a coldness which seemed to numb me.

The man put his hand over my heart, but quickly tore it away again with a cry of terror.

"What is it, George? What is it?" almost shrieked the lady, for his action was so sudden and unexpected that it thoroughly frightened her.

He stood back, and she clung frightened to his arm, as a large blindworm wriggled itself out from my bosom—fell on the ground—and glided away down the hillside into the copse below.